Book design by Caleb Laughlin

ISBN 978-0-578-93593-5 (paperback)

www.caleblaughlin.com

TO MY FAMILY

WHO ENCOURAGED ME TO FINISH MY
ALPHABET BOOK OF INFECTIOUS DISEASES,
DURING A ~~FUCKING~~ PANDEMIC!

A - IS FOR ANTHRAX

WRITTEN AND ILLUSTRATED BY CALEB LAUGHLIN

WINBERRY PRESS

A -ANTHRAX

ALBERT APE HAS ANTHRAX
HIS BLISTERS RAISED AND BLACK.
THIS POOR SOUL WILL NOT SURVIVE
THE WEAPONIZED ATTACK.

B-Botulism

Ben the bear has botulism,
Body cold and frigid.
"Uh-oh," he slurs with outstretched arms,
"My bones are going rigid."

C – COVID

CARA CAPYBARA HAS COVID,
IT'S NOVEL AND UNIQUE.
DRY COUGH, FATIGUE AND LABORED BREATH
MAKE HER BODY WEAK.

D - DIPHTHERIA

DIPHTHERIA'S A D WORD,
THAT MANY RIGHTLY FEAR.
FEVER, COUGH, AND THROAT SO SORE -
LET'S PRAY FOR DEBBIE DEER.

E -EBOLA

ELEPHANT EARL HAS EBOLA.
YOU MIGHT JUST HEAR HIM PLEADING:
"I HAVE A RASH, MY EYES ARE RED,
PLEASE HELP ME STOP THIS BLEEDING!"

F. FLU

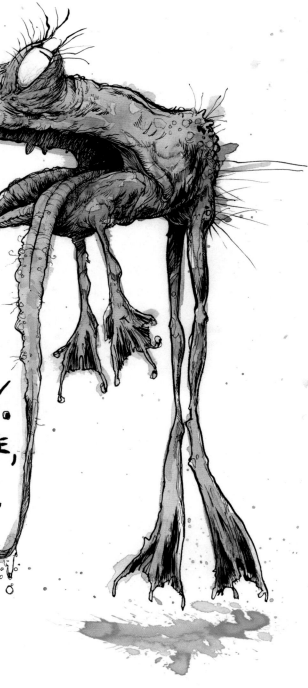

FRED FROG, HE HAS THE FLU,
  HE CAUGHT IT FROM A FLY.
THE SAD THING IS FOR THIS OLD DUDE,
  IT LOOKS LIKE HE MIGHT DIE.

G – GONORRHEA

GILL GOAT'S GOT GONORRHEA,
SO, LIFE IS NOT A BREEZE.
PAINFUL BURNING, TENDER LOINS,
AND FIRE WHEN HE PEES.

H - Herpes

Harriet Hippo has Herpes,
  This mouthful is no feast.
Her itchy ulcers and painful bumps
  Are no picnic for this beast.

I - IMPETIGO

Isaac Ibis has Impetigo,
And plans are now a bust.
His dry, inflamed and sore red beak.
Will soon be covered in crust.

J – JUNIN

JACKRABBIT JEN HAS JUNIN,
HER FEVER WILL NOT STOP.
IT'S REALLY SAD, SHE WILL NOT EAT;
SHE'S LOST HER WILL TO HOP.

K - KERATITIS

BACTERIAL KERATITIS
MAKES KAREN'S EYELIDS WEEP.
IMPROPER CLEANING AND BAD HYGIENE
WRECK THIS KOALA'S SLEEP.

L — LEPTOSPIROSIS

LUKE LEMUR CAUGHT LEPTOSPIROSIS,
WHILE DRINKING FROM A LAKE.
HIS EYES ARE RED, HIS BODY CHILLED,
AND HOW HIS KIDNEYS ACHE!

M - MUMPS

SALIVARY GLANDS ALL RIPE AND PLUMP
AFFLICT MAY MOUSE TODAY.

HER CASE OF MUMPS IS OH-SO-BAD,
SHE CAN'T GO OUT AND PLAY.

N — NOROVIRUS

NIGHTCRAWLER NEIL IS VERY SICK
FROM LIVING IN A GROUP.
NOROVIRUS IS WHAT HE CAUGHT
FROM EATING ALL THAT POOP.

O ORF

OSCAR OTTER'S IN DISTRESS,
BITTEN BY A SHEEP.
NOW THAT HE'S COME DOWN WITH ORF,
HE LIMPS ON SWOLLEN FEET.

P – PLAGUE

POLLY PIG HAS GOT THE PLAGUE,
FROM FLEABITES, LET'S BE CLEAR.
BLEEDING, SHOCK AND TUMMY PAIN –
SADLY, DEATH IS NEAR.

Q - Q Fever

Q Fever is a sickness,
that Quinby Quail's contracted.
"Don't breath that dust," her brother said —
If only she had acted.

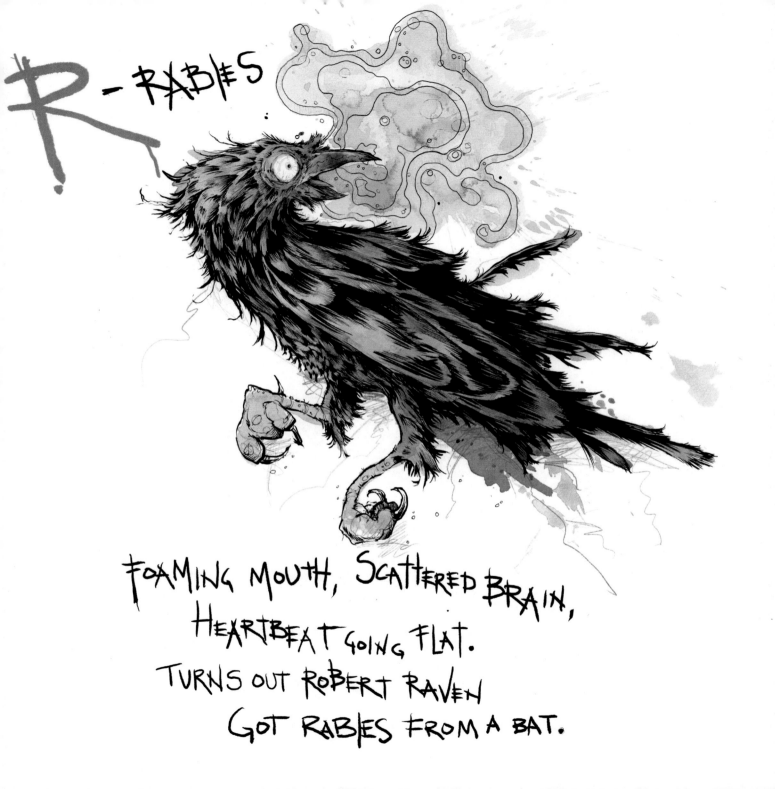

S - SCABIES

IN A LINE, BUMPS OF RED,
CAUSED BY TINY MITES.
SARAH SEAL HAS SCABIES
AND ITCHY RESTLESS NIGHTS.

T - TUBERCULOSIS

TOM TOAD CAUGHT TUBERCULOSIS
WHILST ENJOYING HIS NIGHTLY SOAK.
VOICE IS HOARSE, COUGH IS DRY,
IT SEEMS HE SOON WILL CROAK.

U - UNDULANT FEVER

URSULA THE UMBRELLA BIRD,
   IS STRICKEN WITH UNDULANT FEVER.
HER NIGHTS ARE LONG AND SLEEPLESS EVENTS;
   HOPEFULLY THIS ILLNESS WILL LEAVE HER.

V -VIBRIOSIS

VIBRIOSIS BROUGHT DOWN VICKY
WHO HOARDED TOO MUCH SHELLFISH.
THIS VULTURE'S FEVER AND BURNING STOOL?
THE RESULT OF BEING SELFISH.

W - WHOOPING COUGH

WILL WALRUS HAS BEEN HACKING
FOR LONGER THAN A WEEK.
IF HE DOESN'T CURE HIS WHOOPING COUGH,
HIS FUTURE MIGHT LOOK BLEAK.

X — XERODERMA

XANDER XEME HAS ITCHY SKIN,
A SYMPTOM OF XERODERMA.
IF HIS FEATHERS HE SHOULD LOSE,
HE'LL BE STUCK ON TERRA FIRMA.

Y — YELLOW FEVER

YURI'S GOT YELLOW FEVER,
  A SORE AND ACHING BACK.
HE'S GRUMPY, WEAK AND GETTING STIFF —
  IT'S THE END FOR THIS OLD YAK.

Z - ZIKA

ZONA ZEBRA HAS ZIKA,
WITH KINDNESS YOU SHOULD TREAT HER.
HER JOINTS ARE IN PAIN, AND HER HEAD'S GOT AN ACHE-
ALL THANKS TO A BITE FROM A SKEETER.

ABOUT THE AUTHOR

Caleb Laughlin is an award winning Illustrator who lives with his wife, two sons, two dogs, two cats, seven chickens, three goats, three rabbits and three pigs on a farm in the Pacific Northwest.

A Is For Anthrax is his first picture book.

Made in the USA
Middletown, DE
07 August 2023